For Noah — H.A.B.

STERLING CHILDREN'S BOOKS
New York

An Imprint of Sterling Publishing Co., Inc.
1166 Avenue of the Americas
New York, NY 10036

ISBN 978-1-4549-1881-3

Library of Congress Cataloging-in-Publication Data

Names: Burnell, Heather Ayris, author. | Bomboland.
Title: Kick! Jump! Chop! : the adventures of the Ninjabread Man /
Heather Ayris Burnell ; illustrated by Bomboland.
Description: New York, NY : Sterling Publishing Co., Inc., 2017. |
Summary: In a tale reminiscent of The Gingerbread Man, Sensei bakes a Ninjabread Man to spice up
the sparring in his dojo, and the new cookie is undefeated until a fox appears.
Identifiers: LCCN 2016030676 | ISBN 9781454918813 (hc)
Subjects: | CYAC: Ninja--Fiction. | Martial arts--Fiction. |
Cookies--Fiction. | Humorous stories.
Classification: LCC PZ7.B92855 Kic 2017 | DDC [E]--dc23 LC record available at https://lccn.loc.gov/2016030676

Distributed in Canada by Sterling Publishing
c/o Canadian Manda Group, 664 Annette Street
Toronto, Ontario, Canada M6S 2C8.
Distributed in the United Kingdom by GMC Distribution Services
Castle Place, 166 High Street, Lewes, East Sussex, England BN7 1XU
Distributed in Australia by NewSouth Books
45 Beach St, Coogee, NSW 2034, Australia

For information about custom editions, special sales, and premium and corporate purchases,
please contact Sterling Special Sales at 800-805-5489 or specialsales@sterlingpublishing.com.

Manufactured in China
Lot #:
2 4 6 8 10 9 7 5 3 1
07/17

sterlingpublishing.com

KICK!

JUMP!

CHOP!

THE ADVENTURES OF THE
NINJABREAD MAN

Heather Ayris Burnell

ILLUSTRATED BY
Bomboland

STERLING CHILDREN'S BOOKS
New York

Sensei mixed butter, sugar, and flour. He added extra spice to give it some kick, formed the dough into a stealthy shape, and put it in the oven to bake.

A ginger ninja burst from the oven.

KICK!

JUMP!

CHOP!

"As fast as you can. You can't beat me,
I'm the Ninjabread Man!"

The Ninjabread Man knew
his skills were fresh.

He chopped.

He blocked.

He brushed the chips
off his shoulder and
rolled out of the kitchen.

In the dojo, Raccoon caught a whiff.
"Sugar and spice but something's not right.
It smells like a challenge."

Raccoon searched
for the sugary scent.
"I've been craving a
sweet battle."

CRUNCH! CRUMBLE! CRACK!

Cookie attack! Raccoon couldn't gobble them fast enough.

KICK!

JUMP!

CHOP!

"As fast as you can. You can't beat me, I'm the Ninjabread Man."

"He's a smart cookie," said Sensei.

"He'll crack in the Room of Doom," said Raccoon.
"Look! Cheetah is nipping at his heels."

But before Cheetah
could pounce . . .

The Ninjabread Man was off!

"You are no delicate flour," said Cheetah, "but I taste victory."

"You'd better make it snappy," said the Ninjabread Man.
"Claiming the throne from you will be a piece of cake."

KICK! JUMP! CHOP!

"As fast as you can. You can't beat me, I'm the Ninjabread Man."

"Looks like I cooked up a winner," said Sensei.

"He's a delicious fighter," said Raccoon.

"Watching Monkey defeat him will be a treat," said Cheetah.

The Ninjabread Man slipped into the garden.

Monkey could smell that one tough cookie was on its way.

"You'd better make a break for it," said Monkey.
"I always win at hand-to-cookie combat."

SWAT!

SLAP!

SMACK!

Monkey was swift.

But not swift enough.

KICK!

JUMP!

CHOP!

"As fast as you can. You can't beat me,
I'm the Ninjabread Man."

The Ninjabread Man wiped the icing from his brow.

He shined his candy buttons. He flexed his crisp morsels.

"You are stealthy," said Raccoon.

"You are tricky," said Cheetah.

"And you are full of kick!" said Monkey.

"You have defeated us all. Sparring will be stale no longer!" said Sensei.

"What a mouthwatering challenge," said Fox.

SNATCH!

The Ninjabread Man couldn't kick.

There was no way he could jump. If only he could chop.

"Get your paws off our cookie!" said Sensei.

"Eating the Ninjabread Man will be a snap," said Fox.

The Ninjabread Man gathered his last crumbs of strength and whisked out of Fox's grip.

The Ninjabread Man whipped a licorice rope around Fox. "Eat that!"

"I knew you smelled like you had potential," said Raccoon.

"You are the perfect recipe," said Cheetah.

"We are one sweet team," said Monkey.

"This is the just the spicy batch of ninjas I was hoping for!" said Sensei.

From that day on, sparring had a whole new flavor.